# Dinosaurs Dan

Dinosaur dancing, I see one.
One dinosaur dancing in the hot sun.

Dinosaurs dancing, I see two.
Two dinosaurs dancing in the morning dew.

Dinosaurs dancing, I see three.
Three dinosaurs dancing under a tree.

Dinosaurs dancing, I see four.
Four dinosaurs dancing out the kitchen door.

Dinosaurs dancing, I see five.
Five dinosaurs dancing around a beehive.

Dinosaurs dancing, I see six.
Six dinosaurs dancing and doing tricks.

Dinosaurs dancing, I see seven.

**Seven dinosaurs dancing up to heaven.**

Dinosaurs dancing, I see eight.

**Eight dinosaurs dancing out the garden gate.**

Dinosaurs dancing, I see nine.

**Nine dinosaurs dancing in a line.**

Dinosaurs dancing, I see ten.

**Ten dinosaurs dancing, let's read it again!**